Ghosts of Darke County
IV

Another collection of Ghosts Stories

Rita Arnold

White Dog Books

Cover design by Ron D'Allessandris

Dedication

To my husband Mike who has encouraged my love of collecting and telling ghosts stories.

And to Susie who always knows when I need a push.

To all my friends, new and old who have shared their stories I thank you.

Acknowledgments

I want to thank the fantastic people at DCCA for their support and encouragement for the annual ghost walks.

Most importantly, I thank the readers of my stories. The happiness that I receive from sharing ghost stories with you is beyond description.

You Never Know

My friend and I were talking,
And I found myself in a dare,
He said, he'd take me to a house,
And guaranteed that I'd have a scare!

I thought about it on the way,
And wondered if I'd feel a bump,
He told horror stories I won't forget,
And in my throat arose a lump!

So we went to the old farm house,
Expecting to see a ghost,
And then to my delighted surprise,
I found that the Ghost was my Host!

Milton Arnold, 2006

Ghost

"A ghost wanders among the living, seeing them as a part of another world. The living are uncomfortable in the presence of a ghost. They are trying to understand each other, to communicate."

From a note written by a Vietnam Veteran and left at the "Wall" in Washington D.C.

Introduction

I am pleased to present more ghost stories in this book. I never dreamed that people would be so willing to share their stories. And the stories are from all parts of the county.

Most people do not want to be identified or have the location of the event revealed. To protect their privacy and honor their wishes I have changed the locations and the names. I can assure you that all of these stories actually happened here in Darke County.

Table of Contents

1. The Palace

From 1857 through the present, Greenville has had some type of a building on the northeast corner of Fifth and Broadway.   In 1857 there was the Manasses Creager residence. Then in 1898 on the first floor the Arnold Roll Harness & Saddlery opened in one half of the building and the J. M. Doughty Barber Shop in the other half.

A Mr. Irwin purchased the building at a sheriff's sale from the Creager family. Soon Mr. Irwin demolished the standing building. In the summer of 1900, he began construction of a two story, single building.

In 1900 the Klefeker Grocery Store, owned by John Klefeker, operated out of this location.

Then in 1901 in a giant celebration the Palace Department Store was opened for business. For years this was considered the best place to shop. Years later this store became known as Uhlmans Department store.

A different history book states that from 1885 to 1899 this was The Moore and Winners Dry Goods Store. Regardless of which book is correct, this location has been involved in Greenville history for many years.

This story was told to me by an elderly lady who as a young girl heard the tale from her grandmother who worked at the store in the 1920s.

Claire and her family made their living farming in Darke County. One day while working on the farm, Claire's husband was suddenly killed in a farming accident leaving Claire and the three children totally on their own. They worked the farm as best they could; but it was very difficult for the young family. Claire wanted her children to attend school and have an education; but that cost money. And a day at school was a day away from the farm and doing the necessary chores. But an education was important. Claire spent many hours praying about this situation, wanting to make the best decision for her family.

Ghosts of Darke County IV

When the opportunity came that Claire could have a position at the Palace Department store, she wasn't sure what to do. How would she be able to maintain the farm, keep the children in school, and pay their bills if she did not take the city job? If she took the city job she would be away from the children for a part of each day and the running of the farm.

The owner of the store advised Claire to take the job for a couple weeks and see how things worked out for her and her family. Liking this idea, Claire agreed to a two week trial of the position.

Her section to work in the dry goods store was on the third floor in the shoe department. During those years the windows on the third floor were not covered. People often enjoyed looking out at the town. The employees enjoyed the day light. Not being real sure about the use of electricity the employees never turned on all the store lights until time for the store to open.

One foggy, overcast morning Claire arrived for work a few minutes early. While she was straightening the shoe display she happened to glance out the window. Soon Claire started to daydream about the recent changes in her life and the additional responsibilities she had assumed as a single parent. She was still very worried about making the correct decision, about how to best support her young family and keep their beloved farm.

While looking out the window, Clair heard a woman say "nasty weather out there." Claire turned around and saw a short older lady, with a lined face, slightly stooped over, wearing a long overcoat and a scarf pulled tightly around her face. The older lady was a few steps behind her and looking out the same window.

The old lady continued on saying, "it could change. which is a good thing for people. Remember, good or bad, nothing lasts forever."

Still looking out the window, the old lady stated "that it is good for people to stop and look at the weather occasionally, the older you get the longer you want to look."

Ghosts of Darke County IV

After a short pause, Claire turned to the lady and said that she needed to return to work. Then before Claire could move, the lady looked into Claire's eyes and said "You still have a ways to travel. Don't give up. You'll get there; but always remember where you were."

Claire then walked back to her department to resume arranging the inventory. Suddenly she remembered she forgot to ask the lady if she wanted help finding something.

Claire took two steps back towards the window and stopped dead in her tracks. The lady was gone! Claire heard no footsteps; the floor never creaked. There were absolutely no sounds.

The years passed. Claire managed to keep the farm in spite of some very difficult years. The children matured, married, and had families of their own. Only in later years did Claire tell this story to her family; and then it was with the understanding that no one would repeat the tale.

With a smile Claire often thought of the visit from the old lady. When life seemed the darkest, someone had offered Claire a small ray of hope.

2. The Marching Soldier

For many years now I have heard the story about a soldier marching on Broadway. It usually starts with someone saying "you're probably not going to believe me when I tell you what I saw."

The soldier is usually seen on foggy, misty nights, marching back and forth, back and forth on Broadway. Always on the same block. Always by himself. But do not approach him. If you do, he will march to the end of the block, turn at the corner, head west and disappear. Who is he? Why is he still in that location?

Long before Ohio became a state, this was a wild, hostile wilderness. Living conditions were far from ideal. Harsh weather, freezing cold in the winter, hot in the summer, wild animals, and the American Indians trying to protect their lands all made survival difficult.

Rita Arnold

With the dangerous conditions in this area, life at Green Ville Fort was far from easy or ideal. Many, many soldiers lost their lives in battles. Others died as a result of accidents or disease. Medical care was almost non existent for society back then, especially for people living in what was then considered a wilderness. About all they had to treat the soldiers' wounds or diseases would be any herbs they found, treatments that generations before them had tried, and also plenty of luck.

Many of the dead were buried where they fell. But some of the unfortunate ones who died in battle were left where they fell subject to the elements.

Our soldier dresses like many of the foot soldiers from the 1700's: old worn out clothes, tattered and torn with patches on the pants and an overcoat that covers a thin stooped body. On his head is an old beat up hat with holes. He carries a riffle over one shoulder. As he marches you can tell that he is tired and worn out. He does more of a slow walk than a march. He was not an officer, just a hard fighting foot soldier trying to help his new country grow and develop with opportunities that people could only dream about before.

In the late 1940's and early 1950's Greenville decided it was time to replace the old worn out sidewalks along Broadway. When the construction workers were tearing out the old walkway one block south of the traffic circle, they made a surprising discovery. They found a body inside a coffin. A body which was later identified as a revolutionary soldier. The city made arrangements to bury the soldier in the Greenville Cemetery. But did the soldier not want to be moved?

In a small ceremony the soldier was re-interred in the Greenville Cemetery. There he lies with other Darke County soldiers from various military conflicts. Some people speculate the he is the soldier who is seen occasionally walking on Broadway. Back and forth, back and forth.

Could it be that he is the soldier who walks around the old section of the Greenville Cemetery? But that is a story for another time.

Rita Arnold

3. The Quiet Library

When I was school age, going to the library soon became the greatest influence on my young life.

We did not have a radio or a television. We rarely saw a newspaper. These were considered luxury items. But imagine a place where the books could be read for free! History, fiction, biographies - oh man, I had found paradise.

For years and years there was a female employee of the Greenville Library who began her working career at a very young age. When Margaret (her name has been changed) was in high school she needed to find part time work to help her family. She applied for work at the library and soon found herself working after school and on Saturdays.

Margaret loved her job. After graduation she was offered full time employment at the library. She decided that this would be the perfect situation. She would have a steady income and could help her family.

In those days the library was a very quiet place. Everyone including employees and visitors spoke in a whisper. The employees would walk softly. If a person spoke too loudly, the staff would shush them.

Soon Margaret found herself in charge of the adult book section. She was so happy and proud of her position. Her work reflected her pride. The room was kept spotless. If a table was not in use, every chair was pushed up to the table. With each chair an equal distance from the table.

The shelves were always free of dust. Each book was set in one inch from the edge of the shelf. Most importantly every book was in its proper location. Anyone who worked for Margaret soon found out that she would walk down the rows and check the books. If she found someone shelving a book in the wrong spot, all she had to do was to tap the person on the shoulder, shake her head no, and the book was filed correctly.

Ghosts of Darke County IV

The years went by and Margaret continued to work at the library. She never married and seem very content with her job. Some people said that she was married to her job.

Throughout her life she continued to live at her family's old home, even long after her parents passed away. The house was within comfortable walking distance of the library. She liked the house and the neighborhood. And most of all she loved her job.

The time came for Margaret to retire and the staff gave her a large retirement party. Many were sad to see her leave as they just could not envision the library without Margaret. Margaret promised to visit often.

Over the years she never lost her love for books. Once a week she came to see her friends – both the books and her co-workers.

Then one week Margaret did not come to the library. No one thought anything about this. Maybe she was busy, or had a cold or took a trip.

More time went by and still no Margaret. After work one day, two of her former coworkers stopped at her house to check on her. There was no answer at the front door; so they went around to the back door and knocked. With no answer there, they looked in the window. There on the floor by the table was the still body of Margaret.

One person ran for the sheriff and the other kept trying to open the door. The sheriff arrived and proceeded to kick open the door - finding Margaret dead. The local doctor pronounced Margaret dead due to a stroke.

As the years went by, employees came and went at the library. No one mentioned any unusual happenings. Then quietly those who worked the adult section soon began to compare notes about certain events.

The staff noticed that if the chairs were not returned to the tables they would hear the soft, quiet sound of a chair being moved across the floor to the table. But the chairs were not moved. Just the sound of chairs moving was heard, as if to remind someone to tidy up the furniture.

If an employee incorrectly filed a book, sometimes they would feel a slight tap on the shoulder. This would happen when the employee was the only person in the room. If the employee ignored the tap and continued working, soon they would hear a book fall to the floor. When the staff person went back to retrieve the book, they would find that it was a misfiled book. When the book was placed in the correct location, it stayed on the shelf and there was no more tapping on the shoulder.

Some employees swear that if the noise level gets too loud, they hear a shushing sound as if being told to be quiet.

A long time employee told me that she believes Margaret is still watching over her library and her favorite section.

Rita Arnold

4. The Workers

People in Greenville are accustomed to shopping in the old buildings that line both sides of Broadway. Many of the stores are about the same size on the first floor with two or three stories above that often contain apartments or offices.

The interiors have such character with the high ornate tin ceilings that usually have ceiling fans turning, the old dark woodwork, and, of course, the creaky wood floors that are uneven and fun. This all adds up to making a store special and unique.

During the week most of the stores on Broadway close around supper time. The employees lock up and go home. Some of the stores will have a dim light turned on; others are in total darkness for the night.

Rita Arnold

This story is about one of the stores which has a public area in the front part of the store and in the back half is what is considered the work area.

The work area contains all the usual office equipment, such as a fax machine, a large floor copier, a couple work tables for organizing the jobs, and shelves along one wall that holds the paper, envelopes, and mailers.

This is a busy company; and they always have many jobs going at the same time. They are known for doing excellent work in a timely manner. To be as efficient as possible, the employees will set up the next day's jobs before they go home.

Some days when the employees arrive for work in the morning, they will find a job not completed the day before has been completed. The stack of papers on the copier has been copied. Or they find the paper and envelopes are straightened and restocked.

Is an employee coming in the store at night trying to scare his coworkers? A detailed check of the security cameras and the motion detectors reveal that no one has entered the store or tampered with the security equipment.

Is this being done by a former employee? Or is it someone from years ago who wants to continue working?

The present employees say they never feel afraid. In fact, if the "helper" does not appear for a while, they become concerned. The last person to leave the store will turn out the lights and say "we miss you."

Sure enough the next morning there will be evidence that the "helper" was there.

Rita Arnold

5. The Campfire

Walk along the path to Tecumseh Point when the wind is lightly blowing and listen. Walk very quietly and listen. Do not wear headsets or talk to anyone. Don't sing or hum. Let your mind go blank and listen. Just listen and look and hear. Use your imagination. You may be surprised at what you hear and see.

According to some history books Tecumseh Point is the location (or close to the location) of the signing of the Treaty of Greenville. The only buildings in this area at the time of the signing were the forts that housed the soldiers. This area was wilderness, thick with trees and creeks and streams that ran deep with clear water. The hunting and fishing was plentiful.

The Indians had used this area as hunting grounds for centuries. They fought hard to keep the strangers from taking control of this territory.

The same could be said about the white man who wanted to settle in the area. They were impressed with the beauty of the territory and the plentiful game.

Finally, the two sides reached an agreement and hoped to put an end to the fighting. History states that the men gathered around a campfire for the ceremonial treaty agreement, possibly smoking a traditional peace pipe and then enjoying a celebration feast. This process took weeks.

Over the years, people who have walked near that area have reported seeing in the distance what looks like a campfire. When they reach Tecumseh Point, there is no campfire, no wood ashes on the ground, and no signs of a campfire or the ground having been tramped on. Some people have talked about the faint smell of pipe smoke in that area instead of smelling wood. After a careful inspection of the woods people leave satisfied that there is no fire.

Ghosts of Darke County IV

A few brave souls have sat down on a fallen log just to enjoy the quiet and beauty of that special, historical location. Soon they began to hear the birds singing and the rustling of leaves as squirrels run from tree to tree in the distance. A few years ago you could have heard the fish splashing in the creek.

There is one sound that no one can explain, the distant sound of soft singing with a steady constant beat - a rhythm that goes on and on and on, almost like a chant. No one has been able to understand the words. Those who stay for a while soon start humming with the beat. Others just take off running as fast as their legs will carry them.

Rita Arnold

6. Return to Memorial Hall

Have you heard about the 'people' at Memorial Hall?

Over the years many Darke Countians have visited Memorial Hall for an evening of entertainment or maybe for a school event – a play, a school musical, and years ago a graduation ceremony. We park our cars, rush to enter the beautiful marble lobby, visit with a few friends, and then hurry to our seats as the evening's event is about to begin. How many people take the time to look around once they are inside the building? I mean stop moving completely, slowly look around you at the architecture and the people.

Look carefully at the stained glass windows that grace the front of the building, such rare works of art. Then go up the well worn marble steps, stepping in the same grooves where people have trod for years going to the second floor. Walk around the second floor and listen to the creak of the old uneven wood floor. Again pause and look around the building, this treasure that is Darke County's. Now enter through the tall, heavy wood doors into the balcony seating area and prepare yourself for an evening of enjoyable entertainment.

Something you should know is that not everyone pays for a ticket. But they are always welcome. They attend every performance, every event held at Memorial Hall. They have been attending for years and years.

Some of the local residents have heard the stories about the janitor who is still caring for the building. (I wrote about him in Ghosts of Darke County Book II). He will enter an office during the night and move small objects around that are setting on a desk. He opens and closes the interior doors, and turns on the lights after everyone has gone home.

In the evening, he has been spotted sitting on the pipes in the basement. He is dressed in old coveralls, a flannel shirt, worn lace-up boots, and a well worn old beret style hat that sets at an angle on his head. The clothes remind people of the styles worn in the early part of the 1930s. As he is sitting on the pipes, he is watching the people move about while he wrings his hands together. It is hard to tell if he is cold or nervous; but he just keeps wringing his hands together as he watches the people move about.

Well, last winter a performer came to town for a Saturday night performance. During the afternoon he was rehearsing with the stage crew discussing the stage lighting, the sound system, and the placement of the stage props. He had the show props placed just so and then left the stage for a while. When he returned he noticed that some of the props were moved. The actor did not get mad but he did ask the director to remind the stage hands not to move the props around.

Stage lighting was very important to this show. Many spot lights were used as well as the actor being very active on the stage. The actor went up into the balcony to work with the stage crew on the lighting. Then when he returned to the stage he looked up in the balcony and thought he saw something unusual. He wasn't sure if he should say anything.

Rehearsal continued and the show was a success that night. The actor was pleased with the work of the stage hands.

The next day the director was driving the actor to the airport when the conversation came around to the props. The director informed the actor that all the stage hands were otherwise occupied away from the stage area and they did not touch the props. The director then told the actor about the ghost's stories of Memorial Hall. The actor became quiet, even thoughtful for a while. For awhile the actor just stared out the car window – thinking.

Then the actor told about seeing the shadow like figure in the balcony during rehearsal. The figure was blurry, fuzzy, surrounded by a white mist but clear enough to identify it as a female figure. He wondered why someone was permitted in the balcony during rehearsal. She never squirmed or shifted in her seat. And then without a sound she was gone. The director just smiled as he kept on driving. How should he explain about the lady in white?

7. Another Store with a Story

This story was shared with me by a couple of store employees who did not know that both of them experienced special happenings at different times.

It has always been interesting to me how some people will sense a presence or a being when they are in a building. They may see something, hear a sound, or possibly see an object move. Other people just never see or feel anything – or never admit to seeing or hearing anything. Do ghosts only reveal themselves to specific people? Or are some people refusing to acknowledge the presence of ghosts?

In the early 1900's an undertaker business was established in the 500 block of Broadway in Greenville. In a workshop behind the business the wooden coffins were made using a plain and simple design. Either the undertaker would make the coffins himself or he would hire a local carpenter to assist him. Both men had great pride in their workmanship. Using a hammer, saw, and a plane, the gentlemen built coffins that families were comfortable using for their love ones.

What was nice about the workshop was the large doorway that opened onto the alley. This provided plenty of light and air for the shop. It made for easy delivery of the needed lumber that would arrive in rough hand sawed long planks.

The business earned a good reputation for serving the needs of the Greenville citizens and people from the surrounding area. The families knew that the deceased would be treated with respect and dignity.

A common practice in those days was for the proprietor to have his living residence located above the business. This arrangement was true for Mr. Tate (the name has been changed). For years Mr. Tate worked hard at his business and provided for his family.

Under the business was a basement with a dirt floor and stacked stone walls. There were steep, narrow wood steps that descended from the first floor. The area was used for storage of those items that were only needed occasionally. This basement area was dark and damp due to the fact there were no windows to allow light. Probably few people would venture down into this basement room.

History does not record why, but after about fifteen years the business was closed. Soon another gentleman bought the building and opened a furniture business that was in operation for many years. This business advertised "Up-To-Date Furniture at the Right Price."

The actual building looks like many of the other buildings in that block. A three story red brick building with large windows. This building has withstood the test of time gracefully. There have been very few exterior changes, just some painting of the trim and the replacement of a broken window or a rotting piece of wood trim.

Over the years electricity, telephones, and plumbing have been added to the interior. It was necessary to place the wires and pipes through the floor joists in the basement. This meant that workers were making changes in the structure for the first time ever. People were moving things around in the basement, going up and down the steps often.

A lady told me about the time in recent years when she went down into the basement to bring up some holiday decorations. She turned on the light switch at the top of the steps and walked on down to find the needed merchandise. As she was searching around for the correct boxes she heard footsteps on the stairway. A distinct sound of someone walking down the steps – step – step – step – step. Without looking up, thinking it was a co-worker, she called out that she had found the box and would be right up. As she was talking, she picked up the box and turned around to head toward the stairway. After two steps she suddenly stopped, realizing she was all alone. She hurried up the stairs and found her co-worker in a different area of the store.

Not wanting to be laughed at, she did not mention the episode to anyone. And she was not eager to return to the basement!

A year later after she had completely forgotten the ordeal, she was asked to go to the basement to bring up the holiday stock. She turned on the light switch at the top of the stairway and when down to find the decorations. While down there she heard foot steps coming down the stairway – step – step – step – step. Without turning around she called out that she had found the box and was coming up. When she did turn around no one was there! Needless to say she hurried up the steps and found that all the employees were in the store waiting on customers. Later that year she quit her job and left for college and put this event out of her mind.

A few years later she was talking with someone who was currently working at that store as a stock clerk. This person mentioned that she would hear footsteps when she was alone in the basement. The steady step – step – step – step as though someone was descending the stairway. Both ladies found that they had similar experiences.

No one has seen a vision or had anything else happen to them. They only heard the sound of the footsteps coming down the stairway.

Not all of the store employees hear the steps. Or is it that not all who hear the steps admit to what they are hearing?

Step – step – step – step.

8. The Fountain

Recently Greenville dedicated a new fountain in the traffic circle. This replaced the original fountain that stood for more than 50 years. Before the fountain and the traffic circle, the old county courthouse stood on that location. This wooden building stood for many, many years.

As the county grew, and the need for a larger courthouse became apparent, the old deteriorating building was demolished. Large crowds gathered to watch the demolition of the building.

After the courthouse was completely removed, a group of citizens got together and developed the idea that a landscaped traffic circle would be a nice addition to that location. This would serve two functions: it would assist with the traffic flow and would be attractive to look at.

The original plans were very elaborate for the era with a large circle and four separate grass areas. All of these were to contain trees, shrubs and flowers.

In the final plans the four grass areas were smaller and only contained grass. The circle would have a fountain surrounded by shrubs and flowers. When construction began a large number of citizens would gather to watch the progress of the construction of the circle.

When the fountain was completed there was a large celebration with people from all over the county attending. There were parades, speeches by Lowell Thomas, local and state politicians, and local prominent citizens, all entertaining a large crowd. A holiday atmosphere existed. Again a large crowd gathered in downtown Greenville around the traffic circle.

Over the years, many people used the circle as a landmark. Visitors were told - to go past the circle to the Maid-Rite, or that the James Hotel on the circle, or to go around and north of the circle about half a mile and there you will find The Garst Museum. The Greenville Cemetery is north of the circle and straight south of the circle is the Annie Oakley Park. The circle has helped many people to find their way around town.

For years parades would wind their way around the circle as if the circle were a part of the parade. On holidays the circle proudly displays many American flags. Many people drive to the circle area just to see the flags.

The work on the newest fountain took many months to complete and was watched over by the local citizens with interest.

But were other people watching? There have been reports of a small group of people who would stand off in the distance and watch the work progress. This group consisted of two or three adults and a couple of teenage children. The men were dressed in 1950's style suits, ties, and dress hats. The ladies had on dresses, white gloves, and hats. One of the teenagers wore suit and a hat. The young girl wore a dress and hat. The group just stood quietly in the distance and watched the workers. Sometimes in the evening as the sun disappeared the group was seen standing in the distance looking at the circle. Were these former construction workers who were watching? Or was it a family who came for the first dedication of the fountain and now they want to see the second dedication?

9. The Empty House

Have you ever been in an empty house? How about an empty one hundred year old house? How about an empty one hundred year old three story house?

An old framed house located just south of the Annie Oakley Park stood empty after the owners moved out. The house was for sale and had been on the market for many months.

This was a house that had many, many owners over the years. No one knows of any tragedy or sad event that happened within those walls. The families reported moved because they wanted a smaller place, or they wanted out in the country, or their job transferred them to a different town.

Then one year unfortunately an owner of the house was convicted of a non-violent crime but a serious crime and was sent to prison for a number of years. The other families just came and went but this owner went to a different kind of "house."

One evening around dusk a realtor was showing the house to a young couple. The realtor wanted to show the house in the daytime for better lighting and viewing of the exterior. But the young couple was so eager to see the house and insisted on going that very night.

When the three people arrived at the house, the realtor carefully unlocked the wooden front door. As the realtor began to show the house each room lights were manually turned on as they walked from room to room.

The young couple was very pleased with the house. They started talking about furniture placement, what color to paint the walls, where to place the home office, and what type of window treatments to buy.

Were they so excited that they had finally found a house in their price range that they did not hear the sounds? The realtor told me about hearing the floors creak on the second floor as if someone was walking across the floor. Yet they were all on the first floor.

Then there was the feeling as if someone was watching, watching every move. This feeling continued throughout the house. The realtor felt as if they were always being watched, but he never said anything to the young couple. He did not want them to think that he was crazy.

Then as darkness set in a couple of the closet doors opened and closed on their own, the realtor decided that it was time to leave.

The suggestion was causally made that the three people leave the house and return in the daytime. The next day the group returned and walked through the entire house and all around the yard. There were no creaking floors, no doors opening and closing, and no feeling of someone watching.

Yes, the young couple did buy the house.

Rita Arnold

10. The Park

Everyone who lives in Darke County knows the story of Annie Oakley. Many books have been written about her along with movies and even a broadway musical to tell her story; a documentary has been on public television telling her life story. The Greenville Garst Museum has a fantastic display of Annie's memorabilia.

Every July the county celebrates her life with a huge Annie Oakley festival. Many activities are scheduled involving all ages providing fun for the entire family.

Annie was born in Darke County, not far from Greenville and grew up helping to care for her family. For years she hunted to put meat on the family table. Some of the game she shot was sold to a local grocery store. This helped to provide the family with a small income.

Rita Arnold

After traveling the world demonstrating her shooting skills, Annie returned to Greenville to live out her remaining days.   After a short illness Annie quietly passed away. Annie is buried in a small quiet cemetery a short distance north of Greenville.   There she lies next to her beloved husband.

A few years ago a life size bronze statue of Annie Oakley was dedicated at the south end of Broadway. This is a peaceful setting with the statue near the center of the lot and surrounded by grass and a brick walkway. Tall full trees stand guard between the statue and the nearby buildings. Soft lighting casts a gentle glow at night, as if protecting her. With benches and a gazebo the area is inviting for visitors to stop and spend some time.

Many people drive by the park without looking, really looking, at the statue and the park.

There have been reports of a small woman standing, just standing and looking at the statue. She stands between the trees and the buildings not always in the same spot. She wears a western style hat, a long sleeve blouse, a belted full skirt that stops at the mid-calf area of her legs. On her feet are western boots that come up almost to the skirt hem.

The expression on the lady's face is hard to describe. There is no smile and yet there are no tears. Her gaze never leaves the statue. Then after a short period of time she just fades away. No footsteps are heard; no rustle of leaves as if a person were walking across the grass. The figure just quietly, slowly fades away.

People who have seen this lady report that the expression is something they will never forget. The lady does not look happy or sad, but what has been described as appreciative or satisfied. Then with a slight nod of her head she is gone.

Rita Arnold

11. Another House Story

The stories about the old homes in Greenville are just endless. Each inhabitant wants to share their stories. And I want to hear each and every story.

This is a story concerning a house built in the early 1900's that is located near Tecumseh Point. In fact, you can see Tecumseh Point from the back porch.

Near this house is an old wagon trail that was used back in the 1800's and probably into the early 1900's. Over the years the trail was used less and less. More houses were being built in this area and eventually a house was built on the ground that used to be a part of the old wagon trail.

Some historical articles report that at one time before this area was settled by the white man Indians lived occasionally in this part of the county. In later years the edge of the Greene Ville Fort covered this spot. Many years of hard work to survive the elements were endured by both the Indians and the new comers.

The house in this story sets on a busy section of the street. This is not a house that is located out in the country and isolated but in town with neighbors close by. There are many houses nearby. And just a short distance away is a church, school, and the business district.

Two generations of a family lived together in this house for many years. The teenage daughter was a quiet girl who worked hard in school and at her after school part time jobs. Like many teenagers she wanted a space of her own. After years of sharing a bedroom with her younger sister, her parents finally agreed that the daughter could set up her own private bedroom in the basement.

Oh, the daughter was so excited! Her very own room! She spent hours cleaning and scrubbing the basement room. Then she gave the walls a fresh coat of paint and made curtains for the small basement window.

Ghosts of Darke County IV

The furniture was moved into the basement room along with her clothes, her stuffed animals, the desk and computer.

Just think she could arrange the furniture exactly as she wanted. The daughter found this to be a great setup for doing her home work and just to have some quiet time for herself.

One evening while doing her homework she heard footsteps coming down the basement stairs.

Thinking it was her younger sister coming to spy on her, she called out for her to go away. The footsteps stopped and the girl forgot the episode.

A few weeks later the footsteps happened once again, and again the girl called out for her sister to go away.

Days later when the footsteps happened for a third time, the daughter quietly came out of her room looking for her sister. No one was there. The daughter went up stairs looking for her sister only to find that no one was home. There was a note in the kitchen taped to the refrigerator saying that the family went to the grocery. The daughter decided to put the event out of her mind and to return to her school work.

One evening many days later while in her room she heard muted voices just outside the door. She could not understand what they were saying because the voices were very soft and speaking a foreign language. Carefully, while her legs were shaking she came out of her room expecting to see someone but no one was there.

When this happened a second time a couple of nights later she again found no one outside her door.

Again the daughter decided to forget about the episode and went back to her school work.

There were times when the daughter returned to her bedroom she would find that objects had been moved. Nothing was broken. Just the occasional knick-knack being moved from one location to another.

The daughter started thinking about the events that had happened over the months since she moved into the basement. Suspecting that the house may be haunted she decided not to tell her family. She was concerned that they would tease her or just laugh that she had too much imagination. Her parents would probably say that she reads too many books. But something had to be done.

One evening she sat in the middle of her bedroom with the light turned out, and the television, radio, and the computer turned off. For a few minutes she sat in total quiet. Then softly she said out loud "I don't know who you are but I do know that you do not mean me any harm. Next year I leave for college then you can have your space back."

Years later at a family gathering for the holidays, the talk around the table turned to ghosts' stories. The daughter then decided the time had come to share her experiences that occurred years before in her basement bedroom.

When she finished relating all the events everyone starting talking about other ghosts' stories from different areas around the county. No one else admitted to having experienced any similar events like those that happened in the basement. At least nothing that they were willing to share. Then the daughter looked over at her grandmother who was just sitting there smiling and looking off into space.

The grandmother motioned for the girl to come sit beside her. The two put their heads together and spoke very softly. The grandmother then told her that as a teenage girl she too, experienced the very same events. She told her that the spirits only reveal themselves to the people they trust and care about.

The young girl smiled and gave her grandmother a big hug and quietly whispered "I love you grandma."

12. Meeting the Family

This story was shared with me about a year ago.

The subject of the story was very sincere and eager to tell me of her experience.

On a cold, snowy Christmas night in the early 1960's a young girl went with her boyfriend to meet his family. The event was held in a century-old two story cold drafty farm house located on the edge of town. The young man's aunts, uncles, cousins, and parents were all there.

The men were in the living room playing cards, the kids in another room playing games and listening to music. The women were found in the kitchen sitting on benches around the large wooden table drinking coffee, munching on cookies and visiting. The heat from the wood stove kept the room very warm and comfortable.

As the evening passed the young girl started feeling more comfortable with the surroundings and the new people to whom she was introduced. She joined into the conversations and found that new friendships were already developing.

After about an hour in the kitchen the young girl heard a buzzing sound in her ear. She turned her head around toward the back hallway thinking that was where the sound came from.

Walking down the hallway was a woman who looked to be in her 80's wearing what years ago was called a house dress. It was mid calf length, gray in color, with three quarter length sleeves, and a thin belt at her waist. Her hair was worn back in a bun at the nape of her neck.

The old lady walked slowly down the hallway with a smile on her face as she continued to look at the young girl sitting at the table. The girl did not hear the sound of footsteps. In fact if she was not looking at the hallway she would not have seen the old lady.

Ghosts of Darke County IV

The table conversations never slowed down or stopped. It was like no one else saw the old lady.

The old lady never stopped or hesitated but went directly to the kitchen door that leads to the outside. As she reached for the door knob the young girl said that she should put on a coat because it was cold and windy outside. Then the older lady just disappeared through the door with opening it.

The young girl turned and asked one of the aunts who was sitting next to her if she saw the lady in the hallway. The aunt answered no she saw no one and besides all the ladies were currently present in the kitchen. Not wanting to appear crazy the girl decided not to pursue the matter.

Sadly a few years later the house burnt down. No one else who lived in that house has mentioned a ghostly encounter.

www.ingramcontent.com/pod-product-compliance
Lightning Source LLC
Chambersburg PA
CBHW020142150626
46552CB00021B/1345